Sandcastle.

PHILIP BUNTING

ALLEN&UNWIN
SYDNEY · MELBOURNE · AUCKLAND · LONDON

This is Rae.
Rae loves the beach.

Rae wants to build a magnificent sandcastle.

'Would you like some help?'
says Grandad.

First, Rae and Grandad build
a very tall tower.

Next, they raise the great ramparts.

Then, they dig a deep moat.

They even find a dragon.

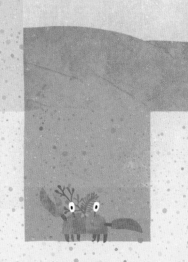

At last, the sandcastle is complete.
And it is magnificent.

Rae and Grandad eat fish and chips,
while the tide creeps closer.

'Do you think the moat will
keep out the sea?' asks Rae.

Grandad says nothing.

'The ramparts will hold the tide, won't they?' asks Rae.

Grandad says nothing.

'Even the tower is gone,' says Rae.

'Don't worry,' says Grandad.
'The sandcastle is still here;
you just can't see it.'

'What do you mean?' asks Rae.

'The sandcastle was made of many grains of sand,' says Grandad. 'Sand that has been here for a very long time. The sandcastle may be gone, but everything that made it is still here, and always will be.'

'I think I understand,' says Rae.

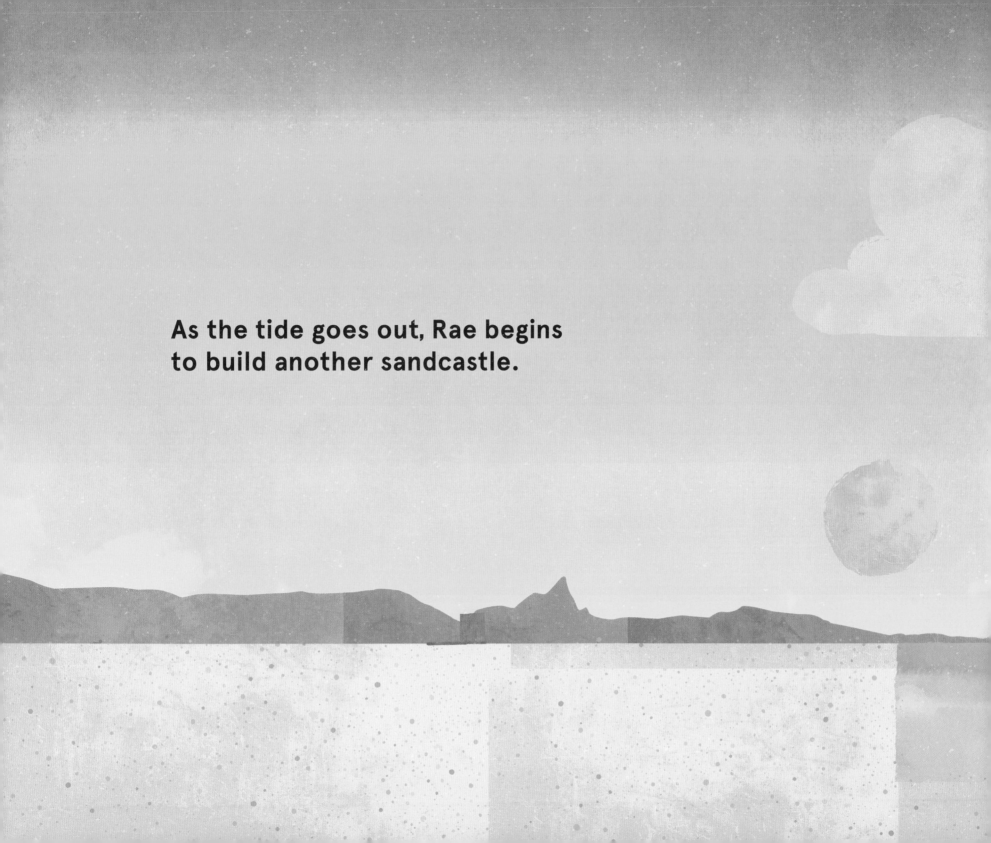

As the tide goes out, Rae begins to build another sandcastle.

And it is magnificent.

FOR GEORGE + IAN

You, me, this book, your breakfast … we're all made from tiny
particles, stuff that has been around since the beginning of time.
We're only borrowing these particles from the enormous universe
that made them. Once we're done with them, the bits that make
us will go on to lead many new existences on Earth, and beyond.

First published by Allen & Unwin in 2018

Copyright © Text and illustrations, Philip Bunting, 2018

All rights reserved. No part of this book may be reproduced or transmitted in any form or by any means, electronic or mechanical,
including photocopying, recording or by any information storage and retrieval system, without prior permission in writing from the publisher.
The Australian *Copyright Act 1968* (the Act) allows a maximum of one chapter or ten per cent of this book, whichever is the greater, to be
photocopied by any educational institution for its educational purposes provided that the educational institution (or body that administers it)
has given a remuneration notice to the Copyright Agency (Australia) under the Act.

Allen & Unwin
83 Alexander Street
Crows Nest NSW 2065
Australia
Phone: (61 2) 8425 0100
Email: info@allenandunwin.com
Web: www.allenandunwin.com

A Cataloguing-in-Publication entry is available from the National Library of Australia
www.trove.nla.gov.au

ISBN 978 1 76029 538 7

Cover and text design by Philip Bunting
Set in Aperçu

This book was printed in November 2017 at Hang Tai Printing (Guang Dong) Ltd., China

10 9 8 7 6 5 4 3 2 1

philipbunting.com